1857

ARJUN CHANDRASEKHAR

ISBN 978-93-89759-84-6

First published in India 2021 by Leadstart Inkstate
A Division of One Point Six Technologies Pvt Ltd

Sales Office:
Unit No.25/26, Building No.A/1,
Near Wadala RTO,
Wadala (East), Mumbai – 400037 India
Phone: +91 969933000
Email: info@leadstartcorp.com
www.leadstartcorp.com

Disclaimer: The views expressed in this book are those of the Author and do not pertain to be held by the Publisher.

Editor: Tanzeel Saiyed
Cover: Ami Parekh
Layouts: Kshitij Dhawale

To my parents and VC.

Contents

About the Author

Arjun Chandrasekhar hails from Palakkad of Kerala. He is a Mechanical Engineer by profession and keeps a passion for writing from his childhood. His first work of fiction, titled The Sophomore Saints: A Himalayan Tale was published in 2015. He has written several poems and short stories in pursuit of his passion for writing. Arjun was bestowed with the title Ambassador of Words in 2018 by Museo de la Palabra, Museum of Words, Madrid Spain for his contributions towards the development of Spanish language and in developing bonds through words between cultures. He is currently working in New Delhi. He is currently developing his new work of fiction titled Vijayanagar.

Chapter 1

The skull, the soldiers and the *sufi*.

They rose from bones,

Of three, once lived and breathed.

Bones charred to dust and smithereens.

One wouldn't reckon the limb from the skull,

Of three, but intact was one – a skull.

Alam Beg his comrades called it

When it wore flesh and breath.

When it housed the fire of thoughts

Like a living hearth.

They formed the formless - forms of the dead.

Not a vestige of the humans that they lived as once persisted in them now.

Only revenge! And a floating soul!

Only the saints saw them; those formless forms,

Only the *sufis* heard their chatter,

Those floating souls.

The conspiracy under the banyan tree

Bheem: What hath our brothers done,

When we were gone,

For, all is there where it had been.

All that struggle is undone?

What folly?

Oh my tamed lions.

 You hang heavy on your own redemption.

Hapless, hapless lot!

All that blood. Sacrifices!

You hapless sheep.

Betrayal bothers! The worst of its kind. The darkest deceit! cried one Alam Beg. He was the lucky one of the rest. The one that was left with his skull. The bravest in the herd.

In those days.

In the days of beginning,

When the khakhi hugged fresh on his high frame.

In those days,

In the forests of war. His white masters may remember.

How Alam Beg fought for a King and Country that was not his.

Like the man-lion of the forest,

Even the beasts humbled.

No less was Bheem. Like the name says.

Many a war have the masters won,

That his muscle and musket helped.

Many a war have the masters won

Against his own lot.

Now we can do no harm to a feather. Think not of vengeance now.

The pinnacle of misery is that vexing hill of hapless – regrets,

We tend to climb it now Kandu – the lesser one, in muscle and musket. He was that feeble breeze that whispered.

He despised the white man like the rest. But the man's core was feeble. The others knew it well.

On that faithful day, when the first shot was fired. His brave brothers had to turn the butter in to iron.

Only then, only then did his slothy fingers listen to that call for the trigger.

Martyrdom has changed little. Getting blown in to smithereens by a cannon fire could do little to what was given at birth

Revenge, roared Alam.

Nothing less

Any flickering compromise may deliver us a death, far deadlier than the one we had espoused!

Revenge, I agree, said the brave voice Bheem.

What folly brothers? Kandu sounded in the chatter of the leaves in the breeze.

Rage is indeed the assassin of thought!

Reckon that we exist no more,

Not at least in matter and form

We are disembodied souls,

We float like feathers

We are hopeless than those hopeless rotting in the white man's holes

But don't you see it brothers, we are at last free

Isn't this what we *seapoys* fought so dearly for?

Rubbish! Rubbish! A traitors feeble utter

Give him no heed brother

Imbecile knows no more

Alam Beg the bravest spoke, when he could bear no more.

Mastan: "Pardon great ones, pardon this humble one. But, if I may speak, I can be light

Who dare speak? Show yourself. If you were born and is yet to be reborn like us feathers Alam roared.

The new voice, he knew, was not a soul.

From behind the tree, showed himself, a tramp.

His robe and beard avowed it loud.

He was a sufi. A holy one.

An endless meanderer, fettered to none.

Forgive my intrusion, revered ones. But couldn't help but speak

I bow before you. The guiding light of thy martyrdom shall lead struggles hereon

….at your feet….at your feet

Bheem: Who are you tramp?

How could you hear what none could hear?

How could you traverse to the other side of winds whisper?

What magic do you hold?

Mastan: I am different my lords.

I listen to what none can listen.

The passing wind whispers to me.

The graves tell tales of the dead.

The rivers and streams sing for me as I pass.

Those like you, disembodied souls that float over me when I nap

Your chatter and cries wake me up

But seldom do I care

Now that what you speak matters

The great struggle matters

Seldom do I listen to the souls chatter

But this one was of the struggle so great

That I couldn't pass

I chose to speak, for this struggle is great

The victor is the master, the vanquished is his slave.

The victor is the master, the vanquished is his slave

Alam Beg: Listen oh tramp who lends his ears to the dead

What good can you bring?

The shabby tatter that you are speak louder

Your words are hollow, be gone!

Mastan: Allow me to quell your doubts, oh great ones.

Even the contempt is given his last words before the gallows

Bheem, Alam, Kandu: So you may speak

Mastan: I woke to hear the lesser ones chatter.

His words that you brave ones despised.

His wavering words – a desperate man's resort

A bastion of lost hopes

I rejoiced to hear the skulls retort

But doubt is a web of intrigue.

The fatal venom that inebriate even the strongest to inaction
and desperation.

Hence, I chose to speak

I spoke, for, I had the light and you had the purpose fair

The marriage of these bring might!

Alam, Bheem, Kandu: You speak well for that tatter and
beard

Speak more. We long to hear

Mastan: Oh great ones, I speak of redemption.

Freedom, and the path un to it.

Freedom!

The same cause that shattered your bodies

And quiver your thoughts even now

Even when you are all undone! Mastan started

Freedom, soldiers! The path to freedom!

Cull the charades and sufi songs

We have no minds to mark them

We are souls

Thou shall speak of the light
That you so promised to show, the great ones sang.

For, they had no mind to bear it long.

The cannons blew it,

Flesh and bones along.

Mastan: Pardon, pardon. My great ones, If I may begin

You are indeed hapless

In the matters of the matter since the cannon thereon

You poor disembodied souls

But indeed in the dimensions and crafts of the spirit

Your heads are high

My lords

Thou shall awake your brethren

In flesh and blood

Those who still live and breathe

and plant in to their shaky heads

The seeds of an impeccable plan for the next struggle ahead

One fought only to win, great ones

One fought only to win

How, asked Bheem.

 Doubt trickled still in to the huge aura of his confuse soul.

Yes, how? Alam sounded the second.

The white man is too smart.

So, like a fox

No plans we make, we poor brown lot

Hold good, before his army of intrigue and seafaring might,
said Kanhu, the doubt-embodied soul.

Mastan: No white man's army is fatal

Than the army of serpents within, these doubts!

You three lords can be the voices of their dreams

And give them a new garland of thought

Incite them to the greatness

Of another struggle great

Tell them, indeed, to tread on velvet this time.

The white man is indeed a crook, beware!

You can be their inner voice

Their eyes and ears in the skies

Where none traverse

There, thou shall stalk and glide

And be their beloved spies

Read the thoughts out of the white man's lords

And pass before they could make the call

Their generals premeditations

Shall be leisure pamphlets for our boys to read on

Ruminate, counteract and at times laugh-on

To pass and act in unison.

Tell them where the whites hide their fire-horses

Their bayonet and blades that bleed us dry

Put the hapless guards to sleep

For our kin to sneak in, plunder, and cease

That you spirits can.

Initiate them to the visions and innovations

From a time yet to come

Teach them the make of metal-monsters

The muskets that fire better.

The rain of blades from a calm, glossy metal ball

That they will call, those in times ahead, grenade

A lot you spirits can commit now

Believe!

If anything bounds, its doubt

Win it, and the war is won

The victor is the master,

The vanquished is his slave.

The victor is the master,

The vanquished is his slave.

Alam Beg, Kanhu, Bheem: you enlightened us great saint.

You are indeed not a simple tramp

We march now to seek thy plan

Mastan: I shall give you a parting *mantra*

It shall ensure victory in our great war

Alam Beg: Kindly reveal great one

Mastan: Its small and beautiful

Like a poem, like a fire, in a two worded breath

say it. The three lords requested.

Jai Hind Mastan gave it to them.

Don't forget, he reminded as they parted.

Jai Hind

Chapter 2

Sowing the seeds

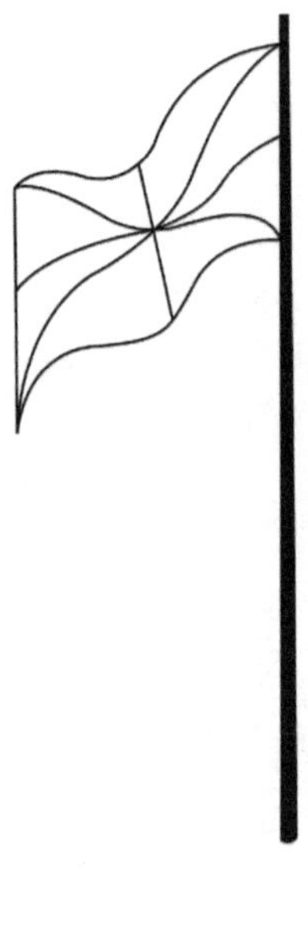

In those days of doom,

When the union jack slowly spread its cold grip on the subcontinent,

Their military camps dotted the landscape in the heart of the north,

Where they held tight,

And down east to the banks of the Bengal blue,

Where his flags fluttered high.

One among them – a camp of camps,

Where they housed the tamed lions like lamps.

One among them, the camp of camps,

Was Ramrahimpur,

It was an oversized golden star in the white man's maps.

A drizzle descended over the camp

Like a boon to the scorched bodies below.

A drizzle the *seapoys* savored as they slept.

Hugging only emptiness, and their rusty muskets.

Like orphan babies in the worst of streets, in a shower,

With none to shade.

But they knew not that the drizzle was not the drizzle that used to drizzle before.

It was a *maya* of the souls, a cover to their descend.

A majestic act from the skies,

 To the enslaved earth below.

Nature applauded with her wet, weary hands, through every drop she wept.

Ram and Rahim. Two *seapoy's*. Two among the tamed, and subdued like sheep.

Ram and Rahim, two *seapoy's* brave.

Brothers,

Friends,

Their village was one,

Where they come from.

They fought and dined as one.

Alam Beg: The two asleep are ideal sheep. For their aura is a flower of light, don't you see

The rest are rust, more dead than alive

The aura is the sign to choose. As so said the sage.

Here we have it in these two

Bheem: yes, indeed. Choose the ones that shine. Wake them now and the whole Hindoostan shall they wake

Kandu: I doubt it still. How to wake those in deep sleep? We are souls, our call is unheard

Our limbs are light and has no form

Alam: We stalk their dreams and speak

Bheem: I agree

✢ ✢ ✢

Chapter 3

The Dream

Never had Ram a bad dream,

It all went into the black hole when a tired man sleep-
thoughts, memories and dreams.

He was a *sipahi*, a warrior. And like his white masters often
say a warrior mustn't sleep

If that was the case he could never sleep.

Then how could he ever dream of dreams.

All the guard and march of the day only killed the Indian
soldier from the night to the next day.

They never slept, those poor tired lots,

They died at nights to a blissful feeling,

And woke up to a new birth the next day.

And in that vortex of birth and death, how could a *seapoy*
even dream of dreams.

As he never slept.

It was so, but, not that night,

When his mind chose to meander free, away.

He saw a hamlet as he walked down a pigmy-hill.

That he reckoned was his place.

Those huts, those trees,

The temple and the groove near.

That tree near the temple that gave shade,

Where their children liked to play.

As he reached the base,

The village was before him clear.

As he closed in,

As his feet creped,

A solo cry was in the air.

A wale, as sober as a tiring bird in a vicious gale.

It was a woman in pain.

It was a mother in pain.

A cry unheard to all else but him.

There was his hut where his old mother lived and died,

Raising him from the child to this man.

The hut was empty when he went for war.

It was alone, like him.

But not now, behold the *seapoy*, it was not alone.

It housed a mother.

No! Not his passed one.

This revered one had a lesser-human radiance.

An aura that mere flesh and blood had not shown.

A thing of skies and not of the humble ground.

Mother! oh revered one

I read thy greatness

That glaring sun in my humble abode of gloom and night speak well what words can't tell

Do speak holy one

What ache your heart so much?

Your sobs rise like a looming cloud over the saga of my warring years

Speak, and I shall I undo it

That rapacious cause, whatever it be

I shall save your tears for the times of glee

And how come your Godly hands be fettered? ... and that revered feet?

Oh God! This sight I cannot take for long

Say the word

Is it a man? Those worst kind

Then to him my musket will speak

Or is it a creature from the other world

A *fauji* as I am

I brush with death, like a farmer with his raven

So for my kind it also matters least

The weary woman spoke like a shiver.

I am the mother of all in the land

For, I am its soul my lad

...of this soil its every pebble and sand

And what cause my bondage is the same for which your musket kills

Your sword culls the weeds that sip from the same chalice that its hounding lips seek

Its parasitic clutches are the fetter on my limbs

Its undone only when that cause is shun

That flag Rama

That flag that gave you your musket and wool

The white man and his flag

The blight behind all the rot and pain in our land

Your brothers tried and failed before

But that you shall outdo

For, you are not alone

You are not alone

I shall give you guides of wisdom and light

Your fallen brothers of course

But not in the former form

Now they are angels, they walk and talk with saints, *sufis* and Gods

They shall twin a plot that may never fail

Believe, obey, and follow their flares

Then the battle is already won

~ ~

Ram: Here I am beneath the green, whispering, umbrella of *bodhi*, this great tree. Reveal oh guides. So said the holy mother. Here you shall shine your light

Alam: Here, he has come. Like our prudent premeditations. Brothers, its time.

Kanhu, Bheem: Aaay!!

Before the *seapoy*'s lifeless eyes,

Those glaring dead, dark, pools,

How deep?

Even death was more alive

It dared, never to venture or seep.

All those wars, death and cries,

All the agonies of mad-years past,

Of man against the man.

They had their toll on the mind, on the soul.

Before the living musketeer appeared the dead; in three,

Floating free in that windless air,

In the world of a tired man's dreams.

So near, so real

The man sighed,

That he forgot to greet.

But within he was all but praise.

Guides, accept my audience.

Please enlighten

Wait not a breath, not another leaf's fall

For, from the white man and the swifts of yonder skies do I seek

The value of time and a beasts phase

When a lot is left to be done

There is a crying mother

Her fetters and cries need be undone

There are fallen kin to avenge

Give me light, a *mantra*, a way forward

The rest I shall see

A soldiers vow

Alam, Bheem, Kanhu: You delight us. So, listen soldier. Seek like a silent grave

They began.

Chapter 4

The *Sufis* war

The might of their race,

The fetters that help them bind,

Its code, its roots are in their thoughts.

My brave soldier.

They hold the book of science,

And salute it before they salute their lord and cross.

And the reward was an indomitable conquerors sail.

They could meander the globe.

They could see and conquer!

They could fetch in fetter,

All that they need.

Alas so wingless are we lot.

 So nonchalant, that we see not what we behold.

Our eyes are hollow, they pass and never hoard.

We see but never learn!

That has made us in to this hapless lot!

My soldier, oh brave one.

What say you?

How does the fire-horse aid the white man and humble our spear and swords?

While their monsters breach our forts, our beasts are dusty things of the past.

How come he sail the oceans and not be lost?

How come his cries travel lands – from Lahore to Delhi? Amritsar to Calcutta?

He pulled the strings and his comrades awakened to slaughter our sheep in that great war before.

They divide and rule, taming our thoughts and senses to his exotic tune.

We behold them all, these albinos games,

But still are a hapless lot.

We behold it all, these white man's games,

But still we learn not.

Ram: what need to be done oh great one? This song boils my blood, like a fire in the stillness and cold. Give me light! Then I shall redeem all sheep. This is a soldier's vow.

Alam Beg, Kanhu, Bheem: then you will be enlightened. Kill your mind but not your soul……and seek, it blooms in five.

GOLD: The first petal.

Alam: The gold rules the world, its forms are many. Yet it is but one. It runs the empires and march the conquering hoards. Like a fire in the hearth of life, it runs it all

Bheem: We lacked it before, we lost, but all is not gone. The great ones of our land have a mantra for us. For, they knew this day would come. It remains still, for the eyes of a selfless few. *Rasayana* is an art to master and rule. The secret formula for the noble metal that rules greed and pride, war and peace, life and death.

Alam: Rama, fetch the metal that flows, *rasa*. Marry it with the lonely herb that blooms in moons silent nights. *Jyan*, those before us had called it. Smear the portion on rock and iron. They shall be made to gold. Thus said great Nagarjuna, the saint of saints. His document was for this day and for all to come.

Kanhu: Men would sell their souls for the metal. I know for I was one oh brother. There you may have your men. We cast our dice first in the white man's board. Now go and spread light!

Ram: your wish, oh revered sirs.

~ ~

Before dawns first light, Ram and Rahim had sneaked out of

the camp. It was no uphill task. The gates were guarded by their brethren. Soon they would put to test the prophesies of the floating souls from Ramas dream. Getting the flowing-metal or *rasa* as it is called in this land was no easy task. A village quack finally helped them. Their kind always kept it. *Jyan* was the riddle. They broke the sleep of the village elder. But even he had the least idea. They had to report back before the first parade in the morning. Somewhere inside, the soldiers started to hear the loud arguments between logic questioning their early day venture chasing a dream. In that defeating hour came to their aid, a song.

"At dawn you reckon it well.

For, its fronds are blades polished by the first glitter of the fresh rays.

It blooms in fire,

The fire of the lotus within.

You see its glitter from the slopes.

Oh, brothers in arms.

You see, you reckon it to be your *Jyan*"

Rahim: And you?

Mastan: Those who don't, call me a mad man call me mastan

The soldiers, brothers, waited not. They were excited to witness it. They crushed the herb on a rock and poured the *rasa* in to it. As they watched, the mixture did its magic on the rock it touched. They saw the gold. It was all that golden yellow. It was all that shine in the morning. Only their doubts still casted shade on its shine.

It could just be a yellow paint on the rock... like the mixture made a golden-yellow die on the rock one of the soldiers *Shak Singh* doubted. The world they lived in had made even the perfect worrier in to a skeptic. Ram ran his dagger on their doubts and a gold flake chiseled out. Now in their hands was the answer. The first petal of what blooms in five was now theirs – GOLD!

Chapter 6

Raheem's Dream: the second petal.

Oh good one. Oh God of your blades.

Your name paces faster than your well-knit frame.

Now hear your part and be awake.

As Raheem looked up, he doubted,

Am I in my brothers dream?

The proud tree, the souls three,

The empty hamlet and this telling breeze.

Or is it...

a dream in a dream

Say you my revered ones.

What do I see?

And what business do I have here?

Is this a dream on my brothers dream?

For, all that he said, I see herein.

Bheem: You owe none for what you see.

This dream, soldier, is yours to see.

Alam: One can't have all five.

The next key is yours.

The clatter of its metal be music to your ears.

You shall see its blossom.

Then spread it through.

Like that merciless conflagration of the woods, it shall spare none.

Our flares shall be lit from its fluttering tongues.

It shall lead our columns in the fight and beyond.

Kanhu: The hardest of iron spit fire, and stand undone by its own thunder.

The white man knows this game better - the harder the mould, the better its done.

Know the alchemy of the male metal

For, you need the man to hold the hearth unflinched.

Its inexorable blows may reap meadows of flames.

But its mother may still hold for spits of fires more.

Smother your thoughts and seek.

This unfolds in two.

Alam: Infernos the worst have ever spawned,

The best of things – living and innate.

That hear shape the metal-male.

Blend charcoal with clay,

And the powdered bark of the *kalpavriksha*

In the hearth of this marriage,

It will be formed.

In that inferno,

The metal-male shall be born.

Fill its hollows with the black powder that fired our cannons from time yet now.

The white man calls this the gun powder.

With this your way will be shown.

~ ~

Under the ghostly shade of an old tree,

Deep inside the woods.

Only the beasts and jackals roam, their Eden, dark and cool.

Away from civilizations inebriating dawn.

Only the natives knew the place,

The white man ventured not.

There beneath the whispering leaves,

Waltzing with the breeze. A cluster of flares showed light,

On the premeditation of a few who dared.

Rahim: They waded the woods and beasts, all the way to join

our cause.

When they heard our call.

They will seek tonight and sneak out before the dawns first light.

Mending the metals our way.

Indian hammers will batter and sway,

In these woods, from the coming day.

Here

The fire-horses that will roar for us in the battle to come, will be born.

They will father their wake.

So, shall the second in the five be unbound.

Ram: Ahoy! JAI HIND.

✛ ✛ ✛

CHAPTER 7

The Mind-Key: The third petal.

Some spend their lives in quest for their dawn.

The one which is for none else but their own.

They travel the plains, climb mountains steep,

Cross the rivers and streams.

All to find that one key,

A charade is life for the weak lot, but a treasure- trove, virgin gold, for those who hold the key.

A mirage it is, an endless seeking, a prospect so bleak.

Until you find it, until you hold the key.

The key is within.

The key is all but within wisdom speaks.

The mind is the charade, the mind is the key

The white man knows well this song.

Divide et Emperale (DIVIDE AND RULE!)

Alam: Beware my brother. Beware of the witch's cast(e) and craft.

That lethal spell, that last feather in her dark, glossy crown.

She cast(e) it in the breeze that come our way,

 And alas!

Brothers split brothers

With blades of grey.

Only in the days that past, they had gifted and hugged each other.

When one said Assalamu alaikum

The other had said Namaste.

She then feeds from our fountains of blood then grow and breed.

Yes!

Yours and mine!

This is the last spell under her sleeve – of religion and caste to cast us apart.

And if this is undone,

We can drive her back to the ocean where she came from.

For this, there is a ritual.

The mantras are the same.

Assalamu alaikum and Namaste

But we shall do it in a different way.

That when Rahim say Namaste Ram shall greet him with that beautiful line Assalamu alaikum.

And then embrace.

In the days to come, in your land, they will call it a word – SECULARISM.

You wouldn't live to hear, yes, but those witches of the day may cast this old spell.

Hence, make the mantra and its ritual your child's play,

Even when the struggle is won.

Benovelance!

✢ ✢ ✢

He may cause you to ponder wild,

With his words - the white man.

His talk is his trade.

His trump in the game.

He spawns a hail of demons to his aid.

These creatures drive astray, us poor sheep.

Our ears sniff his pipe in the air,

And trail it to our ends.

Of benevolence is he talking about?

The benevolence, THE WHITE MANS BURDEN,

To traverse the seas to paint us grey- muddy lots white.

Mind you, this is a lie!

What set his ships to our course was greed. Greed like no other.

Greed, that wild gale that thrust his sails.

You break his lies! You break him plain.

✢ ✢ ✢

CHAPTER 8

Sabotage : The fourth petal

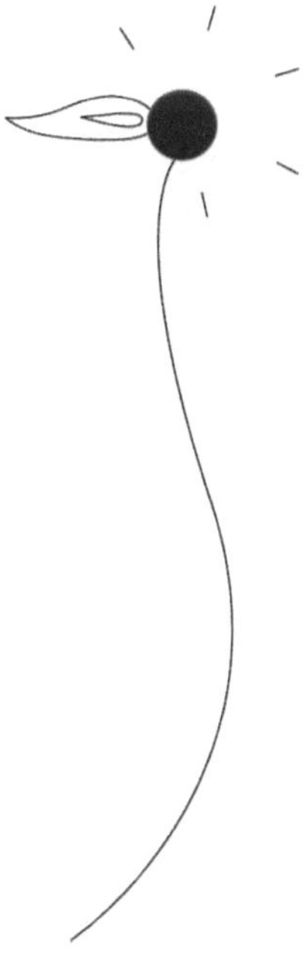

In a dream like before,

In tired, deep sleep.

The men met his guides,

Under that yonder wisdom-tree.

Only this time, they were together,

To see and ponder what's left of the five.

Alam: Greetings brothers.

Ram: Assalamu Alaikum

Raheem: Namaste.

Bheem: The nectar has started to seep deep in to your dead, dark selves.

But indeed now the lamp is only half lit.

Much need to be done and much more need to be undone.

Kanhu: we've come this far! Praise be to the one above.

Alam Beg, Bheem: To the one above!

Call your ears to brace for what is to come.

By the fourth petal you curse his white roots to an ailing death,

And strip his barks bare.

His tree will be but a lifeless tower of fading green,

When all is gone beneath.

Chapter 8.1

The String

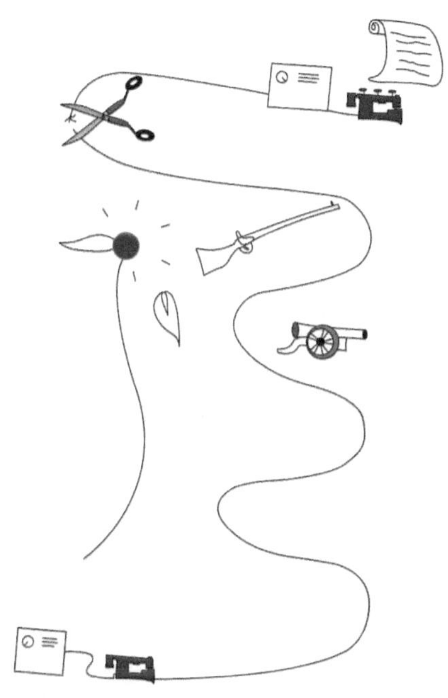

The white man cuddles his magic string.

For, it will save him, he knows,

It had saved his before.

You know when he pulls its tail here,

The cats head at the other end meows.

This keeps his mates known and the governors and generals well informed.

It served him as the key to his triumph,

In that valiant struggle before.

We knew too less to win the war.

Before the die is cast, this time,

Cut his nasty pet in half.

Chapter 9

FIRE: The fifth petal

Commander Union: Your Excellency Lord Benevolent dear sir, dear sir! The lesser men have risen again! The seapoy's your grace! Meerut, Barrackpore, Aarah and Lucknow! A conflagration in the plains!

Lord Benevolent: These headaches, these lesser kind! A scorching de ja vu in my head. We must act fast commander Union. We must act fast and in union. Call him? Where is your Jack?

Commander Union: In the parade ground your grace. Saluting our Raj's union jack.

Lord Benevolent: One must protect what one salutes. Call him; call them all to my oak table. The time is here to ponder the plight, and make plans for another fight.

The HIGHER MEN in conference

Lord Benevolent: What say you Union Jack? And you General White Man.

General White Man: I say what we knew all this time sire. If the Indians are united, they are like fire!

Lord Benevolent Solutions my generals. Speak of solutions and not facts.

Union Jack: The old tune no longer lures them to their fall.

Divide et Emperale has failed! In every tract of this land they greet each other with swapped tongues as a gesture of mutual respect.

Then they hug each other like brothers.

Our undoing begins in this little trick.

They remind us of the fate of that old fox in that old tale,

Every time we try to divide them, and fail.

Lord Benevolent: Then pull the cats tale for Burma.

There awaits our grand army.

A meat-grinder of those rebels of yester years.

They did it before, they will do it again.

General White Man: The string shall call none my dear lord.

The thing is cut in half.

All we have is a broken tail,

in our shaking hands.

Lord Benevolent: What? Good Lords! You must be joking!

General White Man: I wish I were but I am not.

And yes! If you can bear another shell,

They no longer fight with lance and swords!

Lord Benevolent: What do you mean?

General White Man: A magic has given them guns my Lord.

Fire horses! They've ditched the old ways of lance and sword.

And their new guns! Gods of fire and death like ours.

Or even better? God knows best.

The Benevolent White Man and his High Union Jack pondered while the obvious notion tortured their over civilized selves that all cards are played. That all spells cast are undone

But then a last church bell sang in the green plain of his mind.

It said that He is still king of the seas

The English navy rule the seven seas

That his brothers yonder, sailors valiant,

Would cross the blue and help.

The Benevolent White Man and His Union Jack followed that ringing within.

He remembered that faith always helped him.

It may do it again.

The armada

75

Eighteen ships readied their sails,

In an island yonder,

All dawn and no dusk there, some believe.

From a port of pomp and glee.

The sailors readied, as their countrymen, brethren bid adieu.

Heroes they cheered for those sailing aboard.

Because their mission was redemption.

Their fellows lay in ruins

In that land of spices, rajas, snake charmers and music.

Those Indians do know magic mate!

A young sailor said.

Or else

How could they pull this off?

The maggot on the yester-rebels corpse hasn't finished his meal

And now again they have rose?

The English lion mauled these apes before

Our cubs played with their skulls

Our boots trampled on their dead pride

Dead like tuna in our plates

And now we sail to quell them again?

I wonder, I wonder, How and why?

Alam Beg: I see the English fleet. That serpent of the seas.

In sails the English put their faith. All cross, behold, we can't be wrong.

There is an army in their wombs.

A canister of fire and thunder waiting to spill on our shores... to douche the conflagration that we, so struggling, cast upon.

They have an army in their wombs to undo the magic that we have done.

Bheem: No! it can't be! We are magic! We are souls!

They lend us ears, the sea and the storm.

We act now or fade to where the dead dwell, never to come.

Chapter 10.1

The Storm

JAI HIND was the name of their breath and sigh.

JAI HIND, the name of the storm they spawned.

The throb of their selfless thoughts twinned thunder and light.

That every block that made those ships were arrogance and racist blight, made their jobs lite, fanned the ire of the sea gods burning bright.

For, these earthly matters, feeble and worn, could stand no light and storm.

The tides played to the tunes of the pounding gale.

One sailor, ignorantly young for the seas,

Felt that he heard a song!

In that clatter of the heavy drops,

In the maddening hiss of the storm.

...in the waves that manned their deck like a play.

In every drop, in every strand of that revolting air, he felt he heard a song!

Bandeeee......Mataram......bandeeee......mataram....

As if it came from another world. He wondered *what is this song?*

He wondered, even more, later, when he found his drenched frame in a no man's island far north.

The storm had taken the ship and crew. The redemption was shipwrecked to the depths of the ocean.

The lucky ones ashore, cared less to think and mourn,

For that priceless peninsula in the east,

That was now lost.

Independence

Lucknow was a sea of clamor,

-the winners claps and muskets thunder.

In Arra they fought the white men,

Spared their wives and children, like good men.

Faizabad, Meerut and Delhi, then it cut like a sword down south,

Bayonets and swords, fire horses and cannons cried battle-cries in Tamil, Marathi, Telugu, Urdu... So, diverse as it may sound, but it was all but one.

A resonation of their brethren in the north!

But even when it was all won,

Indians were Indians, they could do no wrong.

Those who surrendered, those white men,

Now all torn and worn.

They were spared to seek their soil,

In all the ships that float.

With a promise this time, indeed, of a safe sail and no storm.

Their women, with their pride and honor intact.

The children, unharmed, fed and merry.

Families, together, along.

When they left the shores, the soldiers cared for a happy wave of adieu.

We are Indians they thought. How can we be rude?

How can we be unjust and wrong?

Chapter 11.1

The Last Dream

The night after all that was over,

Parties, victory parades,

Dances, speeches and feasts of glee,

That singings about all that was gained.

Below the waltzing flames of the city ablaze,

They slept - the two who cast the die at first, Ram and Raheem.

They found themselves in a dream!

It was not theirs.

It couldn't be.

Not of Ram. Not of Raheem.

For, they were together in this dream.

At the base of that fateful tree.

We won. They cried like lads as they met their masters - the floating souls.

The three as thick as thieves, the blessed ones.

The fetters are slit, the freedom is won!

Our venture ends here

we belong not to this world

The dead we are

We be gone

But before we part. We cling a code to our adieu, my lads

The white man, he Is gone and freedom is won

But the white - the oppressor - may take other forms to dwell amongst you,

Never to be gone!

So, mark our words for the days to come.

See him in the communalist, those who split us in parts and halves

He hides in the bosom of that demon called caste

You slain the demon, you slain him too

He is in the grin of a corrupt saheb

In the tears of those who sleep empty at nights

You feed those mouths, you build his tomb

That towering mountain of filth that he has left remain.

Now the soldier be the meticulous scavenger till the job is done

Now the soldier be the midwife, a mothers solace, for the new nation in womb

Remember the fetters, the pain and tears

After all that we have won

This torch, its priceless flame and light, should you pass before you go

In hands able, brewing with warm blood young

Stronger hands may man it then

Yet stronger may come to hold

Its guiding light may serve not just the blessed upon this land, but the whole world, in days to come

So, God may help you brave ones, Adieu

Alam Beg: JAI HIND.

Bheem: JAI HIND.

Kanhu: JAI HIND.

~ ~

Away, in the calm shade of some tree, in an old pilgrims route to places holy and free, a sufi sat with a smile. He was no sufi. He was no saint. He was perhaps the souls of all souls.

THE END

✢ ✢ ✢